W9-DIN-044

3 1160 00459 0670

For Caz
M. E.

For Wendy
S. H.

Text copyright © 2000 by Max Eilenberg
Illustrations copyright © 2000 by Sue Heap

First edition 2000

Library of Congress Cataloging-in-Publication Data
Eilenberg, Max.
Cowboy Kid / Max Eilenberg ;
illustrated by Sue Heap. — 1st ed.
p.   cm.
Summary: A young boy has difficulty getting to sleep because
his toys seem to need so many hugs and kisses at bedtime.
ISBN 0-7636-1058-5
[1. Bedtime — Fiction. 2. Toys — Fiction. 3. Fathers and
sons — Fiction.] I. Heap, Sue, date, ill. II. Title.
PZ7.E3443 Co 2000
[E] — dc21   99-054076

2 4 6 8 10 9 7 5 3 1

Printed in Hong Kong

This book has been typeset in A T Arta Medium.
The illustrations were done in acrylics, watercolor, and pencil.

Candlewick Press
2067 Massachusetts Avenue
Cambridge, Massachusetts 02140

Cowboy Kid

When this little cowboy
looked like this,
his father called him
Cowboy Baby. . . .

But now he's grown to
look like this, Sheriff Pa
calls him Cowboy Kid.
YES SIRREE!

Max Eilenberg

illustrated by Sue Heap

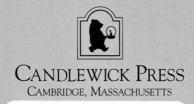

CANDLEWICK PRESS
CAMBRIDGE, MASSACHUSETTS

Cowboy Kid
loved Texas Ted with all his heart.

YES SIRREE!

And with all his heart he loved
Denver Dog and Hank the Horse.

When Sheriff Pa said it was time for bed,
Cowboy Kid gave each of his friends
a great big hug and a sleeptight kiss.

Then Sheriff Pa gave him his very own
great big hug and his very own sleeptight kiss
and tucked him safely in.

"Nighty night, Cowboy Kid," said Sheriff Pa.
"Off you go to sleep now."

But Cowboy Kid didn't feel like sleeping.

NO SIRREE!

I think, he thought, that everyone
might like another kiss.
So he kissed them all again.

Then Cowboy Kid got out of bed.
I think, he thought, that everyone
might like to be a little bit warmer.

So for Texas Ted
he found some socks.
And for Denver Dog he found a scarf.

And for Hank the Horse
he found a special blanket,
just the right shape for a horse like Hank.
Everyone looked much warmer now.

Cowboy Kid snuggled back in.
"Aren't you asleep yet?" called Sheriff Pa.
"Not quite," said Cowboy Kid.

Then Cowboy Kid sat up.
I think, he thought, that Denver Dog
might be lonely on the far side of the bed.

So Cowboy Kid moved him closer.
Only now Hank the Horse
was on the far side of the bed.

So Cowboy Kid moved everyone again.
"Go to sleep now," called Sheriff Pa.
"Almost there," said Cowboy Kid.

But then Texas Ted fell out of bed.

"Oh!" cried Cowboy Kid.

He gave him a great big hug.

"Poor Texas Ted," he said.

I think, thought Cowboy Kid a moment later,
that Hank the Horse and Denver Dog
might like a hug as well . . .

and everyone might like
another kiss, and . . .

"Cowboy Kid," said Sheriff Pa,
walking right in.
"Why aren't you asleep?"

"I can't sleep,"
said Cowboy Kid,
suddenly feeling tired
and tearful.
"Everyone needs
so many kisses."

"My darling Cowboy Kid,"
said Sheriff Pa, "my Cowboy Baby . . ."
He bent down and wrapped Cowboy Kid
and Texas Ted and Denver Dog
and Hank the Horse
tight together
in his arms.

"Let me tell you a secret,"
he whispered.
"One kiss is all you need."

"Just one?" asked Cowboy Kid,
as Sheriff Pa tucked him in again.
"Just one," said Sheriff Pa.

He leaned over and
kissed Cowboy Kid.
Just once.

"One kiss . . ."
murmured Cowboy Kid,
as quiet as quiet can be.
"Everyone might like that."

"Everyone might—
tomorrow," smiled Sheriff Pa.
"But now it's time
to close those eyes."

And this time Cowboy Kid
didn't say anything,
because he had already
fallen fast asleep.

YES SIRREE!

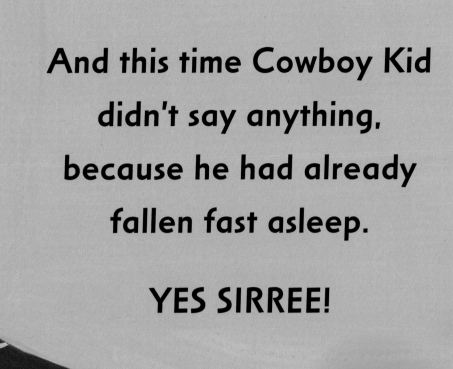